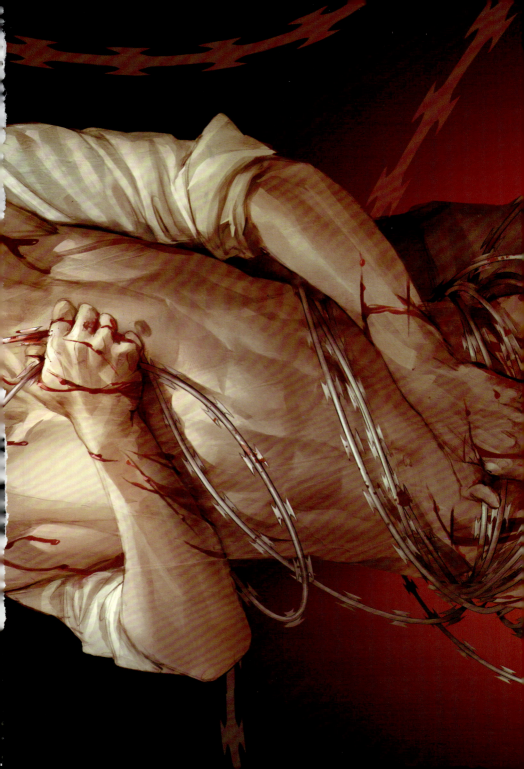

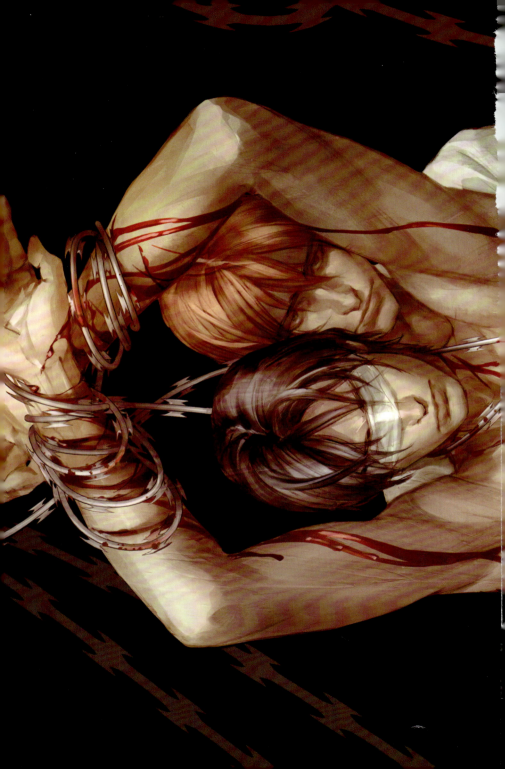

In These Words

volume 2

Comic
TogaQ

Script
Kichiku Neko

Guilt | Pleasure

INDEX.

3 — in these words
229 — wrapped around your finger
253 — nolo contendere

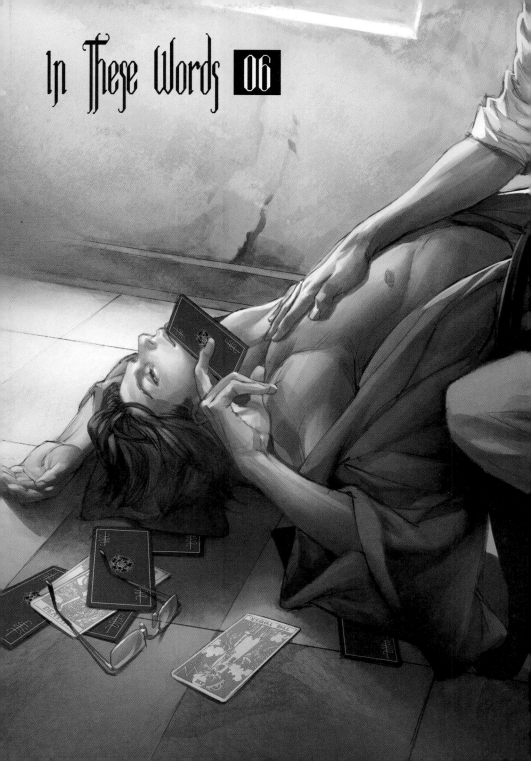

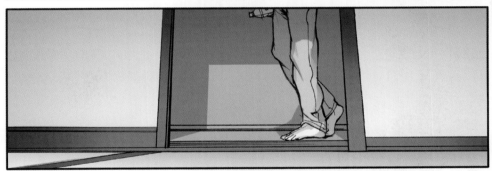

WE'LL START OVER

THIS SHOULD BE OUR HONEYMOON, AFTERALL.

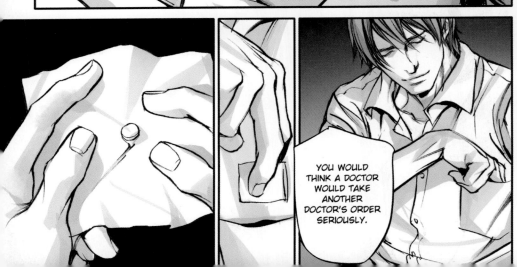

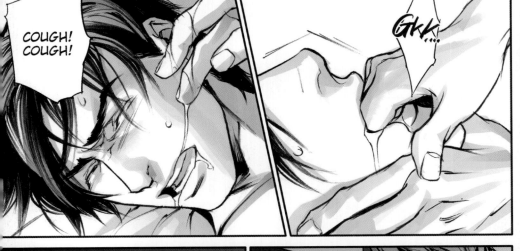

WHAT THE HELL AM I THINKING...?

DAMN IT!!

......

LET GO.

BETTER THAN THE ALTERNATIVE, GIVEN YOUR SITUATION, RIGHT?

YOU SHOULD ACCEPT AFFECTION WHEN SOMEONE GIVES IT.

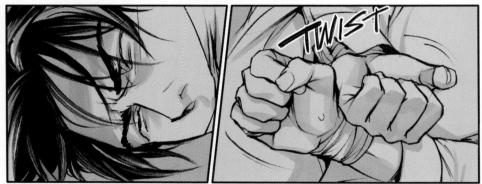

HOW DID HE KNOW THE CODE?

ONLY YOU, IWAMOTO-SAN AND THE CHIEF KNOW THE COMBINATION.

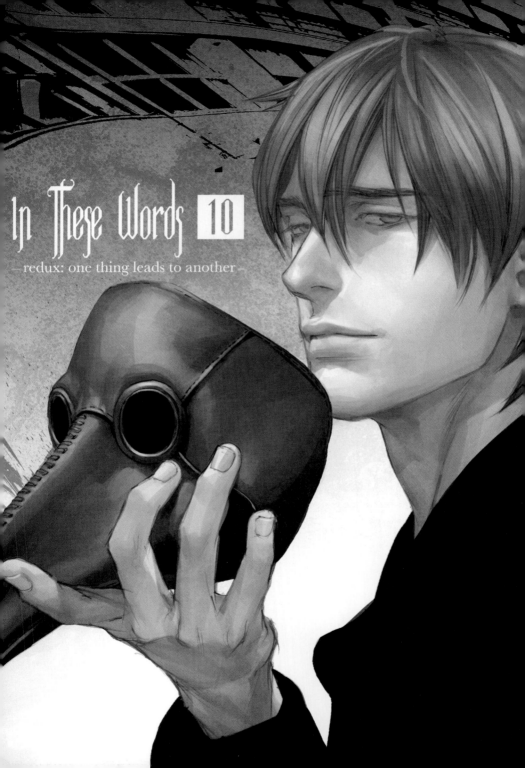

-15 Months Earlier-

RIGHT.

THEN IT BECOMES A MATTER OF APPEASING HIS EGO. AFTER HIS RITUAL'S COMPLETED AND HE CAN'T DERIVE ANY MORE PLEASURE FROM IT, HE CHALLENGES THE AUTHORITIES.

THE LIGATURE MARKS ON THE VICTIMS ALSO SHOWS THE NEED FOR THIS MAN TO CONTROL EVEN THE TIME OF DEATH.

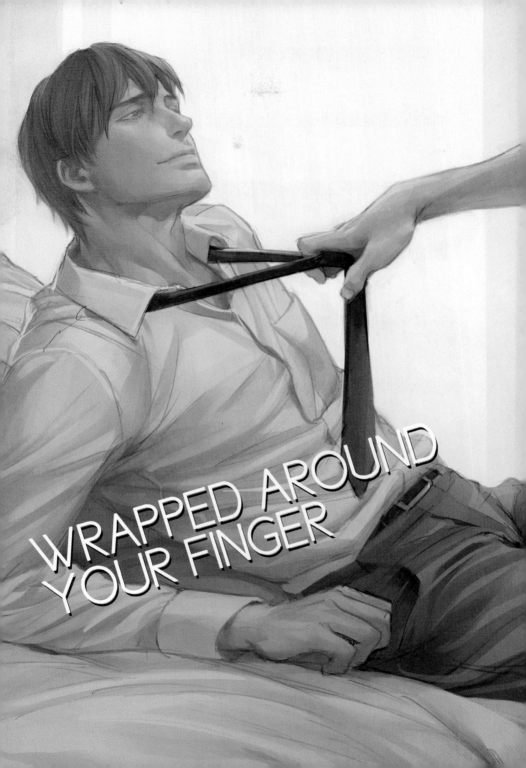

LOADING

EXTRA

NOLO CONTENDERE

In These Words Vol. 2

Illustration//TogaQ
Story//Kichiku Neko
Editing//Mycean
Layout+Lettering//TogaQ、501

ISBN 978-1-62548-017-0

No part of this book may be reproduced, displayed, modified or distributed without the express prior written permission of the copyright holders.

© 2010-2020 Guilt|Pleasure.
www.guiltpleasure.com